THUNDERBIRDS
ARE GO

™

At the bottom of the ocean a deep-sea mining machine made its way along the floor cleaning up pollution. Inside it, a lone scientist Ned, chatted to his only companion – a potted plant!

"This is the job for us, Gladys! No drama…"

But no sooner had he spoken than a klaxon sounded and all the monitors flashed red. There was only one thing for it – Ned screamed!

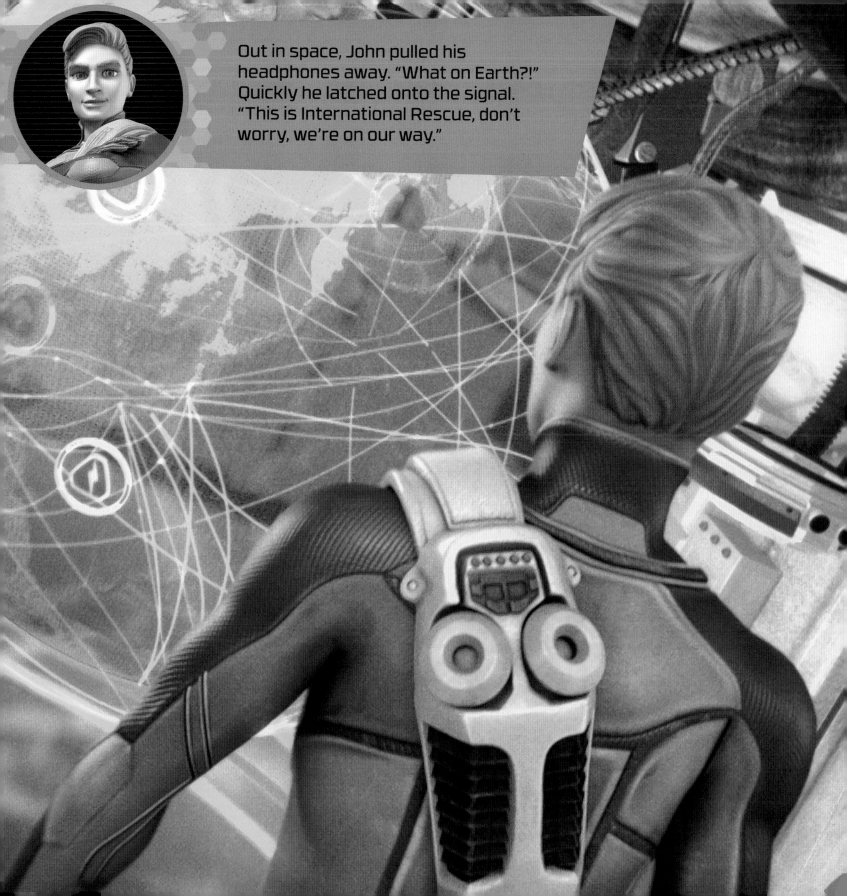

Out in space, John pulled his headphones away. "What on Earth?!" Quickly he latched onto the signal. "This is International Rescue, don't worry, we're on our way."

5 4 3 2

1

Virgil and Gordon raced to Thunderbird 2. "You can't waste any time on this one. If the mining platform breaks apart, so will the tanks of poisonous pollution Ned's been collecting!" warned John.

"F.A.B. We'll save both the crew AND the toxic waste," replied Virgil.

John spoke to the head of the mining company while his brothers raced their way to the rescue.

"I can assure you no one is more anxious to see that toxic waste recovered than us. We'll be ready to take those storage containers away the moment you recover them," said Hector Ambro, head of Hydrexler Mining.

"What does your company do with the pollution?" asked John curiously.

"Oh, it's all very technical, we process it in our state of the art facility," replied Hector dismissively, before abruptly ending the transmission.

Immediately Gordon's image replaced Hector's on screen. "We heard every word. Was it us or did he seem a bit off? I think we need to find out a bit more about him. I know who can help."

Gordon quickly called Lady Penelope who knew all about Hydrexeler and Hector Ambro.

"Oily fellow, isn't he? Let me see what I can dig up." She called off just as Gordon and Virgil touched down at the rescue site.

"Here we are, better go strap in," Virgil told his younger brother.

Thunderbird 4 launched from Thunderbird 2, diving into the water below.

Gordon had no problem finding the machine below the waves - it was massive! He made contact with Ned to find out how severe the problem was.

"I told the boss we were going too deep, but he said the planet depended on me! Now I've got no steering, no pressure regulation, no life support, nothing. And we're on fire! In other words, GET ME OUT!" Ned shrieked.

Gordon had to keep Ned calm if he was going to be able to rescue him.

"Don't focus on any of that. Let's just focus on getting you out of there!"

Gordon knew he had to put the fire out first. He told Virgil his plan to open one of the hatches and flood the rooms that were on fire.

"Won't that damage the pressure system even more?" Virgil questioned, hovering above the water.

"One problem at a time," Gordon replied grimly.

He used one of Thunderbird 4's claws to open the air-lock above the fiery compartments. Soon the flames were engulfed by the water and the fire was out.

Before he could try the next stage in his rescue plan though the huge machine began shifting.

"It's not me, it's moving by itself again!" cried Ned.

Gordon watched as the mining platform turned in the water. He saw there was another problem to add to the list – it was heading to the edge of a huge abyss.

He relayed the new problem to his brother.

"One problem at a time remember, Gordon," Virgil calmly replied. "Let's get Ned out of there first."

In the meantime John and Lady Penelope were updating each other on their investigation into Hydrexler.

"All of this seems odd. When I analysed his call I noticed a hidden algorithm which I've seen once before in the work of The Hood. If it is him you need to be careful Lady P. If he thinks you're on to him, he won't stop at anything to get rid of you," John warned.

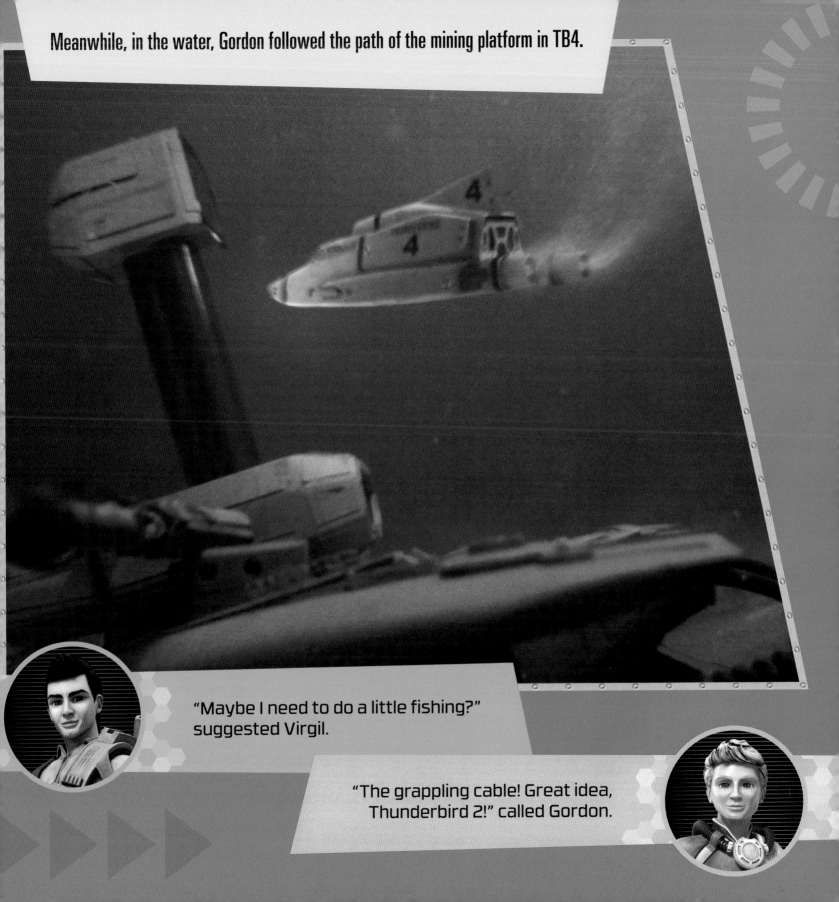

Meanwhile, in the water, Gordon followed the path of the mining platform in TB4.

"Maybe I need to do a little fishing?" suggested Virgil.

"The grappling cable! Great idea, Thunderbird 2!" called Gordon.

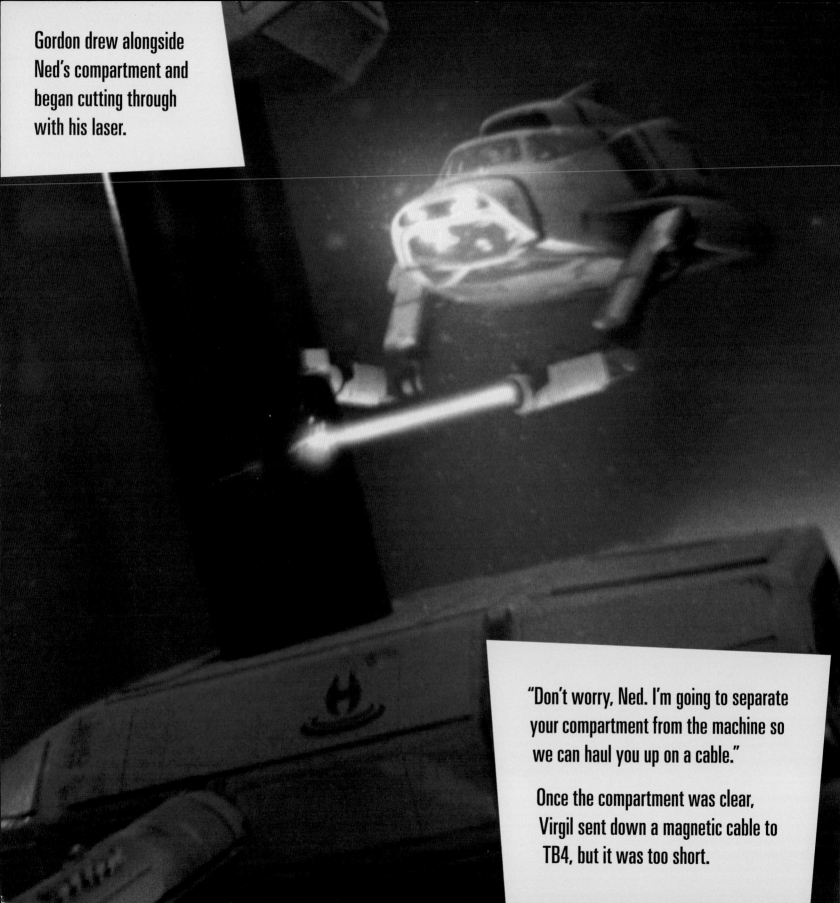

Gordon drew alongside Ned's compartment and began cutting through with his laser.

"Don't worry, Ned. I'm going to separate your compartment from the machine so we can haul you up on a cable."

Once the compartment was clear, Virgil sent down a magnetic cable to TB4, but it was too short.

"Up for a game of catch?" called Gordon. Using TB4's grappling arm, he threw the compartment that he had removed from the machine towards the magnetic cable. Luckily it caught it on the first attempt! Ned screamed all the way to the surface, clinging on to his only friend - the potted plant.

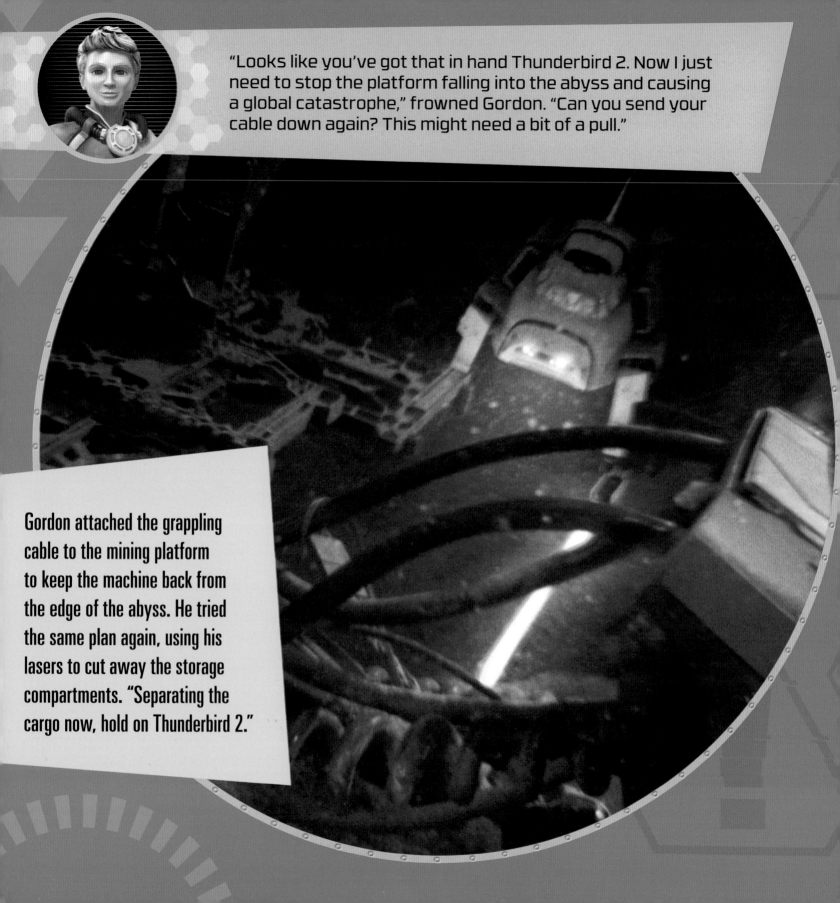

"Looks like you've got that in hand Thunderbird 2. Now I just need to stop the platform falling into the abyss and causing a global catastrophe," frowned Gordon. "Can you send your cable down again? This might need a bit of a pull."

Gordon attached the grappling cable to the mining platform to keep the machine back from the edge of the abyss. He tried the same plan again, using his lasers to cut away the storage compartments. "Separating the cargo now, hold on Thunderbird 2."

The cable was pulled taut and Virgil could feel himself being pulled closer to the water.

"Any chance you could hurry it up a little?" said Virgil. "I'm not really in the mood for a swim."

Gordon tried to speed up as he noticed cracks beginning to appear in the toxic compartments. They were going to burst.

Time was running out for the brothers, and Gordon knew there was only one thing to do.

"I can get a better cut on the cargo section if I go out in my suit," he told his brother.

"You'd have only three minutes before the pressure cracks your suit," warned Virgil.

"Plenty of time!" Gordon joked. He jumped on board his aqua scooter and using his portable laser began cutting away the final toxic compartment. The pressure cracks were getting bigger and Thunderbird 2 was practically in the water.

"Thunderbird 2's no longer going to hold. The platform is taking me under. If you're going to cut it free, it has to be NOW!" said Virgil urgently.

The compartment finally broke free.

"Well done, little brother. Now get back inside Thunderbird 4 and let's figure out how to get that toxic waste back to the surface!" Virgil called in relief.

But it wasn't as simple as that . . .

Gordon watched in horror as the platform tipped over into the abyss - with TB4 still attached! He raced after it on his aqua scooter. He and TB4 disappeared from sight and contact as they plunged into the abyss.

"Come in Gordon . . . Gordon!" Virgil called desperately to his brother.

"Sorry TB2, I had a sub to catch! Let's head home!" said Gordon as he and TB4 rose to the surface free from the mining platform.

With the brothers safely back home, John and Lady Penelope updated them on their investigation.

She had discovered that Hydrexler were secretly owned by The Hood who had been storing all of the toxic waste in a water treatment plant.

"As far as we can tell, The Hood's plan was to secretly contaminate the drinking water supply then charge a fortune to clean it up," John relayed from Thunderbird 5.

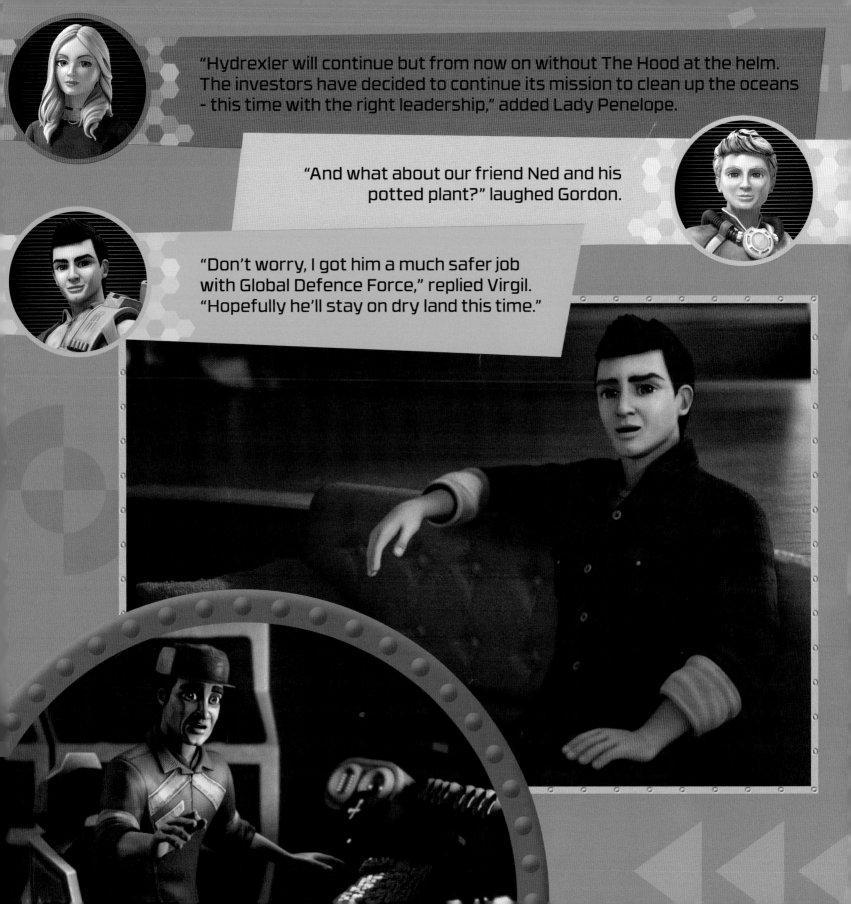

"Hydrexler will continue but from now on without The Hood at the helm. The investors have decided to continue its mission to clean up the oceans - this time with the right leadership," added Lady Penelope.

"And what about our friend Ned and his potted plant?" laughed Gordon.

"Don't worry, I got him a much safer job with Global Defence Force," replied Virgil. "Hopefully he'll stay on dry land this time."

LOOK OUT FOR THESE OTHER AWESOME THUNDERBIRDS ARE GO BOOKS

OUT NOW!

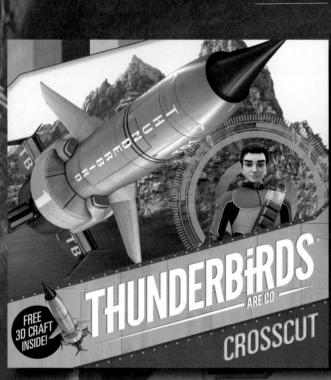

FREE 3D CRAFT INSIDE!

THUNDERBiRDS ARE GO
CROSSCUT

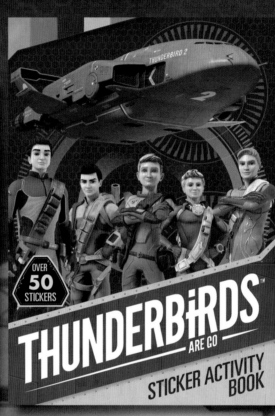

OVER 50 STICKERS

THUNDERBiRDS ARE GO
STICKER ACTIVITY BOOK

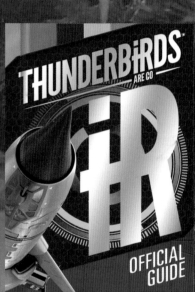

THUNDERBiRDS ARE GO
OFFICIAL GUIDE